THE FRESHMAN

THE FRESHMAN

K. R. COLEMAN

MINNEAPOLIS

Darby Creek
A division of Lerner Publishing Group, Inc.
241 First Avenue North
Minneapolis, MN 55401 USA

For reading levels and more information, look up this title at
www.lernerbooks.com.

The images in this book are used with the permission of: iStockphoto.com/Dmytro Aksonov; iStockphoto.com/Purdue9394; iStockphoto.com/PhonlamaiPhoto; iStock. com/sumnersgraphicsinc.

Main body text set in Janson Text LT Std 12/17.5.
Typeface provided by Adobe Systems.

Library of Congress Cataloging-in-Publication Data

Names: Coleman, K. R., author.
Title: The freshman / K.R. Coleman.
Description: Minneapolis : Darby Creek, [2018] | Series: Kick! | Summary: After he joins the varsity soccer team, high school freshman Iggy Baptiste tries to ignore the upperclassmen's hazing, but when his best friend Malcolm becomes their target, he might have to take action.
Identifiers: LCCN 2017010748 (print) | LCCN 2017032837 (ebook) | ISBN 9781541500303 (eb pdf) | ISBN 9781541500204 (lb : alk. paper) | ISBN 9781541500297 (pb : alk. paper)
Subjects: | CYAC: Soccer—Fiction. | Hazing—Fiction.
Classification: LCC PZ7.1.C644 (ebook) | LCC PZ7.1.C644 Fr 2018 (print) | DDC [Fic]—dc23
LC record available at https://lccn.loc.gov/2017010748

Manufactured in the United States of America
1-43652-33469-8/16/2017

The book is dedicated to Malcolm and
Auggie—neighbors and teammates.
Go, Minneapolis United!

IGGY and Malcolm walk across the soccer field. The sun is barely up, and the ground is still wet from last night's rain. The air smells of worms and mud and freshly cut grass. It's the last day of high school soccer tryouts— the last day to prove themselves.

The boys are the first to arrive. They head to a wooden bench and pull on their soccer cleats. Iggy's are cheaply made and are starting to feel too tight. He's gone through three pairs of cleats in the past year. Last summer, at the beginning of his eighth-grade season, he was one of the smallest players on the field—wiry and short with a round, baby face. But now he's long-legged and lean and ready for his freshman year.

"You think Coach Yuro will post the teams tonight?" Malcolm asks as Iggy squeezes his left foot into his shoe.

"It would be torture to make us wait. I probably won't be able to sleep if he doesn't."

They know they'd be two of the best players on the junior varsity team, but a few spots are open on varsity. The Edison High School soccer team struggled last year, and Coach Yuro is looking for new blood. Iggy thinks Malcolm probably has a better chance since last year's goalie struggled. The senior goalie's name is Joe Smalley. That's kind of funny because the guy is huge. He's well over six feet tall, and he grew a thick beard over the summer.

Malcolm pulls his foot onto the bench and ties his mud-covered shoe. His cleats used to be bright red, but during the first day of tryouts, the older guys kept calling him Dorothy and asking him to click his heels. After that, Malcolm did his best to take the shine off and turn them from red to a dirty brown.

"Speaking of Coach Yuro." Iggy nods to a tin equipment shed as the varsity coach steps out pulling a wagon filled with orange cones. He waddles across the field—a short, big-bellied man with hair that sticks up in jagged spikes. All week Iggy has tried to read the coach's face, but it's like a slab of concrete—pale and unmoving. He doesn't smile, and he never seems to be looking when Iggy does something good. The coach definitely notices when Iggy does something dumb, though, like jumping for a header and getting nothing but air or tripping over an untied shoelace.

"You need any help?" Iggy shouts. He feels weird just sitting there.

Coach Yuro grumbles something under his breath, shakes his head, and continues setting up the orange cones.

"I guess not," Malcolm says, grabbing a soccer ball out of his bag and bouncing it on the ground.

Iggy nods at the net. "We should get going." He wants to practice before the upperclassmen arrive. They've been going after

Iggy and Malcolm and the other freshmen all week, doing everything they can to give the younger guys a hard time on the field. The returning varsity players wanted to get in the heads of the younger players, and it worked. Iggy knows that today he and Malcolm have to stay in the zone to have any chance of making the team.

As the two freshmen head toward one of the nets, Coach Yuro roars. "What are you two doing? Get off the field. I'm still setting up!"

They scramble back to the sideline, and both yell "sorry!" at the same time.

"Yikes," Malcolm whispers. "Someone's not in a good mood."

"I've heard he's never in a good mood." Iggy points to an open space near the equipment shed. "Let's practice over there."

They grab their water bottles and set them about twenty-four feet apart, the width of a soccer goal. Malcolm stands in the middle and stretches his arms and legs.

"Ready?" Iggy yells, backing up.

"Ready!"

Iggy sets the ball down, steps back a few more feet, and then surges forward. The ball jumps off his foot. It goes high and bends to the right. But Malcolm seems to know exactly where it will go before it even leaves Iggy's foot, and he leaps up and easily plucks the ball out of the air.

Iggy has been working on this shot all summer, and Malcolm has been working on stopping it. They've practiced nearly every day together in the alley behind their houses.

"Put some power behind it," Malcolm says as he rolls the ball back. "That was pretty soft."

"Just warming up." This time, he kicks the ball harder. It doesn't bend or go high. It rockets straight at Malcolm. The goalie barely gets his hands up in time to knock the ball down.

"Better!" Malcolm grins and rolls the ball back to Iggy. It's the same grin that greeted Iggy nearly ten years ago when he first moved next door to Malcolm. Iggy was new to this country, and his English wasn't good, but he understood Malcolm perfectly when his new neighbor knocked on the door with a soccer ball tucked under his arm.

They've been playing soccer together ever since—either on a school team or in the alley behind their houses. Malcolm is becoming a great goalie, and Iggy is finding his way as a striker. For Iggy, there's no better feeling than scoring a goal.

Iggy turns and looks when he hears voices echoing from the parking lot. He watches as a group of seniors make their way toward the field. Compared to most of those guys, he and Malcolm look like little kids, but on the field, size differences don't matter as much. They've been able to keep up with the older guys so far, but today they need to do more than just keep up.

Iggy looks at Malcolm. "Ready?" Iggy wants to prove that he can kick the ball as hard and as fast as any of the upperclassman.

Malcolm nods. Iggy takes a few quick strides and blasts the ball. This time, it goes low and bends to the left—not where Malcolm was expecting it. He dives, but the ball streaks past Malcolm's fingertips. To Iggy's horror, it hits Coach Yuro right in the groin.

COACH Yuro bends over and sucks in his breath. He's still holding onto the metal handle of the wagon he was pulling. When he drops it, there's a clanging sound as it hits the tarred path next to the equipment shed. Iggy watches as Coach Yuro's face turns purplish red. It no longer looks like stone. It looks like hot lava.

"I'm . . . I'm . . . sorry," Iggy sputters. "I didn't see you there."

Coach Yuro doesn't look up. He just takes huge breaths as a couple of older players come up behind Iggy. One of them snickers. "Oh, man. What did you do?"

"It was an accident. Do you think I should get him some ice?"

The guys burst out laughing. He didn't mean to be funny. He just didn't know what else to say. He can't believe this happened on the last day of tryouts.

Coach Yuro, still bent over, glares at Iggy.

"I'm really, *really* sorry about that," Iggy says again. "I didn't see you."

"Ten laps," Coach Yuro says. "Now!"

Iggy turns and runs. Yesterday he felt as if he had a chance to make the varsity team, but now he wonders if he'll even make JV.

He passes a group of players and tries to ignore their pointing and laughing. "I'd run all the way home if I were you!" someone shouts.

Iggy sees the JV coach walk onto the field. Coach Julio is the opposite of Coach Yuro. He's younger and taller. He's in good shape, and he seems to enjoy his job. Iggy watches as Coach Julio and Coach Yuro stand together on the field, talking.

Soon Coach Julio blows his whistle and waves everyone in. Iggy jogs over with his head down. He stands in the back of the group, and he wants to smack the guys in front of him who keep glancing at him and laughing.

"Quiet!" Coach Yuro demands. Iggy notices that the coach doesn't look quite right as he bellows out the plan for the day—he's obviously uncomfortable, and his face is still red.

"First, we'll run some drills, and if you do them right, we can scrimmage. Got it?"

They all nod their heads.

"I didn't hear you!"

"Yes, sir!" everyone shouts.

"Good." Coach Yuro looks at his clipboard. "Listen for your names. Anderson, group one. Britton, group two."

Iggy realizes the names are being called in alphabetical order, but his name, Baptiste, was skipped. He waits. *Maybe there's another list*, he thinks. But soon everyone is in a group except him. He stands by himself.

"Coach Yuro?" Iggy says.

Coach Yuro starts to walk away, but then Coach Julio steps in. "I think Baptiste here was missed."

"Oh, was he?" Coach Yuro squints at his clipboard. "Baptiste. Group six." He points.

"Get over there."

Chad Swenson, the varsity captain, is standing in front of the orange cone where Iggy's group has gathered. Iggy catches up as Chad is pulling his long hair into a bun on top of his head.

"Hurry it up, freshman!" Chad shouts at Iggy. "Did you get lost?"

Iggy joins the small group around Chad.

"Listen up," he says. "As captain, I report to the coaches. So you need to impress me if you want to make varsity." He looks at Iggy and the two other freshmen standing next to him. "But ankle biters never impress me much."

Some of the older guys laugh, and Chad flashes a crooked grin over brilliant white teeth.

"Line up!" he snarls. "You three first." He places the three freshmen in front of the line.

"Go!" Chad shouts.

The first kid in line runs down the field, but he isn't sure what to do. Chad kicks a ball and hits the freshman in the back of the head. He stumbles and falls to the ground.

"Oops," Chad laughs. "Not too impressive."

The next guy in line heads down the field and turns, ready for a pass. But Chad blasts a powerful kick that streaks past him.

"Wake up out there!" Chad yells. He looks mad.

Iggy is next. The varsity captain smacks Iggy on the back and grins crookedly. "Go!" he yells.

IGGY cuts quickly when he sees Chad kick the ball. He stretches and stops it with the tip of his foot, then turns and smoothly passes it back.

"That's how you do it!" Chad looks surprised that Iggy got to the ball. "Next!"

Coach Yuro blows his whistle a few minutes later, and the groups shift. Coach Julio is in charge of the next station. He stands with a stopwatch in his hand and a smile on his face. "All right, guys. Let's have some fun!"

At noon it's finally time to scrimmage. The sun is beating down and the air feels swampy, but Iggy tries to ignore the heat. The scrimmage is his last chance to show off his skills at tryouts.

The coaches put the returning varsity players on one team, along with the rest of the upperclassmen. Everyone else takes the other side of the field.

"This is going to be tough," Malcolm says to Iggy as they put on red jerseys. "But at least we're on the same team."

"You'll be fine."

"I don't know." Malcolm watches the older players line up. "I'm half the size of most of those guys. Check out their goalie—he looks like he's seven feet tall."

"But you can fly," Iggy says. "That guy can barely move."

Malcolm smiles. "And you can score. So let's do this!" Coach Yuro blows his whistle, and the scrimmage begins.

The action starts slowly—both teams seem bogged down by the heat. Then Iggy breaks up a pass. He runs down the sideline, somehow sneaking his way through two huge, broad-shouldered varsity players. Iggy pushes ahead, dribbles in toward the net, and takes a shot. The ball curves to the left and heads for the upper corner. Smalley has long arms, but his movements are heavy, and he can't reach it in time. Goal!

"Beautiful shot!" Coach Julio shouts from the sideline. "But I want to see you pass more out there. Play as a team!"

They line up on the field again. Chad Swenson and another senior dominate the play. They pass the ball back and forth, keeping it away from defenders. Iggy sees Malcolm get ready. He takes a few steps forward, spreading his arms and wiggling his fingers as if getting ready to take flight.

"Come on, you've got this," Iggy says under his breath.

Chad moves to the front of the net and fires a shot. Malcolm is ready. He flies through the air, grabbing the ball and pulling it into his chest.

"Yes!" Iggy shouts. "Superman!"

Malcolm boots the ball down the field. Iggy is open, but Chad hustles back to catch up and takes the ball away. The senior is fast, and a second later, he's bearing down on

Malcolm again.

Iggy chases the play. He's just a few feet behind when Chad takes a booming shot, but once again, Malcolm is there. He stops the ball and makes eye contact with Iggy, who races back down the field, cutting toward the sideline. Malcolm kicks a perfect pass right to him. Iggy dribbles, cuts to the middle, and passes to a sophomore in front of the goal. The sophomore puts it away for the team's second score. They're ahead by two!

"Nice passing!" Coach Julio shouts. "Keep working together out there. Keep your eyes open."

As the teams line up again, he can hear Coach Yuro yelling at his players. "No one is guaranteed a spot on the varsity team! No one. Not even if you've been on this team for the past three years. Show me you deserve to be here before I replace all of you!"

Iggy notices that Chad's face is red and his bun has started to come undone. He looks angry, and when he gets the ball, he runs hard into Iggy and knocks him down. He jumps up and manages to poke the ball out of bounds as Coach Yuro blows his whistle for halftime.

"Nice stops," Iggy says to Malcolm as they gulp water. "Looking good."

"Nice goal," Malcolm replies.

"Pretty good for freshmen, don't you think?"

"We're holding our own," Malcolm says with a grin.

In the second half, the older guys start to play rougher. There's more tripping and even a few elbows thrown, but Coach Yuro doesn't stop the scrimmage. He watches from the sideline, his face unreadable.

Soon Coach Yuro blows his whistle and switches the goalies. Malcolm heads to the opposing net, and Smalley takes over for Iggy's team.

The last thing Iggy wants is to face his best friend, but he knows that Malcolm can take care of himself. If anything, Iggy wonders if he can score on Malcolm. He's stopped shot after shot at tryouts, just like they practiced in the alley all summer. Malcolm has reflexes like a cat.

Chad scores twice on Smalley in the second half to tie the game. Coach Yuro checks his watch. There can't be much time left in the scrimmage. Iggy passes to a teammate and then speeds forward. The teammate quickly passes it back near the left side of the goal. He sees Malcolm move out, ready for the shot. As Iggy pulls his leg back to kick, he's pushed from behind and falls to the ground. Chad stands over him, hands in the air as if it was an accident. But Coach Julio doesn't buy it. He blows his whistle and calls for a penalty kick.

Malcolm looks out at his friend. They've faced each other over and over, but this time is different. The coaches are watching, and teams will be decided this afternoon.

Iggy takes three strides and kicks the ball. It goes high and bends to the right. Malcolm moves toward the ball, but when he leaps to knock it down, his back foot slips. He doesn't get enough height, and the ball skips off his fingertips and into the net.

Iggy is stunned. His stomach falls. He knows Malcolm would've stopped it if he hadn't slipped. This isn't how he wanted to win.

"We would've won if we had a full-size goalie guarding the net," Chad says loudly. Iggy can tell Malcolm heard Chad. His friend walks off the field with his head down.

Everyone gathers around the coaches. "The results will be posted tonight," Coach Yuro says. Then he shrugs. "But nothing is written in stone. Don't think you can stop working if you make varsity."

Iggy notices a couple of older players give each other uncomfortable looks, but Coach Yuro's words give Iggy hope. If he doesn't make varsity today, maybe he'll still have a chance to move up later.

MALCOLM and Iggy are quiet as they gather their things. "Your foot slipped," Iggy finally says. "I've seen you stop a million shots like that before."

"It would help if I were as tall as Smalley," Malcolm says, shoving his water bottle into his bag. "I look like I'm in sixth grade."

Iggy frowns at his friend. "Don't let those guys get in your head."

"I wanted to do better." Malcolm zips up his bag and sighs.

"Well," Iggy says. "At least you didn't kick Coach Yuro in the groin."

Malcolm pauses. Then he shakes his head and laughs.

"You made an impression, that's for sure,"

Malcolm says, and Iggy laughs with his friend.

As they're walking home, a black convertible filled with varsity players squeals past them, inches from the curb. Malcolm and Iggy jump back.

"Freshmen!" Chad Swenson shouts from the driver's seat as the car rushes by. Everyone in the car hoots and laughs. Iggy watches them turn onto a street a block away. He has a bad feeling about lingering on the sidewalk.

"Let's go to Herbie's before we head home," Iggy suggests. "My dad finally got Herbie to install a slushy machine."

Malcolm nods. "Sure."

The bells on the door at Herbie's ring as they walk inside. Iggy's dad is restocking the candy rack and smiles up at the boys. He's been managing this little gas station convenience store for the last five years, and he hopes to buy it when Herbie retires later this year. It's his dream to own a business.

"How were tryouts?" he asks.

"Iggy scored two goals during the scrimmage."

"And Malcolm made some amazing saves," Iggy adds. "He stood strong against the varsity players."

"Slushies on me!" Iggy's father grins and nods at the new machine. "Just got it hooked up last night."

"Thanks!" Malcolm says as he and Iggy grab cups.

Iggy's father takes out his wallet and goes to the register. He's never allowed Iggy to take anything free from the store.

Malcolm blends two flavors together— grape and green apple. The combination turns a strange brown color. Iggy fills his cup with cherry and takes a sip of the sweet, cold drink.

Iggy's father pours himself a cup of coffee from a thermos. "Let me make a toast," he says. "To future soccer victories!"

Iggy and Malcolm clink their plastic cups against Mr. Baptiste's coffee mug.

"Is there anything you need me to do?" Iggy asks his dad. He's been helping out all summer, working a few shifts each week with his dad. He even has a shirt hanging in the back room with his name embroidered on the chest.

"No, no," his dad says. "You two go home. You worked hard at tryouts today. And it's your last week of summer break. Go have fun or just relax."

The boys say their good-byes to Mr. Baptiste and head out of the store. They haven't gone far when they hear a car creeping up behind them. Iggy turns around and sees the black convertible again.

"Hot out here today, huh?" Chad says, pulling to the curb and stopping the car.

"Yeah." Iggy takes a sip of his slushy. He wonders why Chad stopped and unbuckled his seat belt if he wasn't going to get out.

"Maybe this will help!" One of the guys in the backseat pulls out a slingshot and a water balloon and hands it to Chad. Chad stands up, pulls back on the slingshot, and fires at Malcolm. The slingshot sends the water balloon whizzing through the air, but Malcolm's reflexes are too good. He ducks, and the balloon flies past Malcolm and nails Iggy in the shoulder. Water splashes his shirt and face, and his slushy splatters on the sidewalk.

Chad reloads and fires another water balloon that zips inches past Iggy's face. As Chad reaches for another missile to launch, Malcolm takes the lid off his slushy and flings the cold, brown liquid at Chad. It splatters across his face and hair and drips down the steering wheel and front seat.

"Look what he did to my car!" Chad screams, wiping the slushy out of his eyes. "Get him!"

"That was probably a mistake," Malcolm says. He and Iggy turn and run.

Water balloons fly past their heads. One smacks Malcolm in the back—he staggers but stays on his feet. They keep running, cutting down an alley near their houses.

"This way." Iggy jumps over a small wooden fence and hides behind a stack of cardboard boxes in someone's yard. Malcolm follows him. A dog barks, and the sound of footsteps and voices gets closer.

"Come here, little freshmen. Come out, come out, wherever you are!"

Iggy and Malcolm don't move. They don't even breathe.

The footsteps move past them, followed by the sound of a car driving slowly down the alley.

"We don't have time for this," Chad says. "I've got to head back. I have a meeting with Coach Yuro in an hour. I'll take care of that little freshman later." Car doors slam, and the convertible drives away.

"I'm dead," Malcolm says. "I threw a slushy at the varsity captain. In his car."

"He fired water balloons at us with a slingshot," Iggy says, rubbing his shoulder. "That hurt. He deserved it."

"Maybe we should switch schools," Malcolm says. "Try out for a different team."

Iggy thinks his friend is only half joking. "I think we're too late for that, and I'm not going to switch schools to avoid Chad Swenson."

The conversation is interrupted by the sound of a screen door opening and slamming shut. Iggy sees two girls about their age step onto the back porch near where the boys are hiding. One girl has short, cropped hair that is bleached white and accented with streaks of pink. The other girl has long dark hair tied into two braids. They're both holding ice cream cones.

The girl with the braids peers into the shadows. "Malcolm? Iggy?" Iggy realizes it's Maya Pham. She lives on the other side of the alley behind the houses where Malcolm and Iggy live.

"Why are you in my backyard?" the other girl asks.

"We were, uh . . ." Malcolm starts to explain but stumbles.

"Playing hide-and-seek," Iggy finishes.

"What are we, six?" Malcolm says under his breath.

The girls lean against the deck railing and look down at them.

"This is Lainey," Maya says. "She's new. Lainey, this is Iggy and Malcolm. We're all going to be freshmen this year."

"I just moved in," Lainey says, nodding to the stack of boxes behind the two boys.

"Where'd you move from?" Malcolm asks.

"California." Lainey licks at the dripping ice cream she's holding.

"Oh," Malcolm says, and Iggy can see him searching for something to say. "Do you surf?"

Lainey laughs. "We didn't live by the ocean. I'm from the edge of the desert. I played soccer instead."

"Soccer!" Malcolm says, standing up. "Us too."

"You guys want ice cream?" Lainey asks.

"Sure." Malcolm and Iggy climb the wooden steps to join the girls on the deck. Lainey returns with two more cones.

Iggy licks his ice cream. "How did your tryouts go?" He remembers seeing Maya and Lainey on the field the day before.

"I don't know," Maya says. "There's a big group of returning players, so there are only two open varsity spots. It's going to be tough."

"You have a chance," Lainey says. "You were one of the best shooters out there."

"Thanks." Maya looks at Iggy and Malcolm. "This girl knows how to set up a play. I couldn't have scored without her."

"Whichever team we end up on, we're going to be unstoppable!" Lainey says. The girls laugh and touch their ice cream cones together as if they're making a toast.

Lainey turns to Malcolm. "What position do you play?"

"Goalie." Malcolm looks as if he might say more, but instead, he just takes a huge bite out of his ice cream.

"Iggy plays forward," Maya tells Lainey and then says to Iggy, "You're a striker, right?" He's surprised she knows that. They haven't hung out for a while. When they were younger, Maya used to join Iggy and Malcolm for games of soccer in the alley, but during middle school, she didn't seem to have time anymore.

"Yup, striker."

"When do you find out about teams?" Malcolm asks.

"Tonight at six," Maya says, taking her phone out of the back pocket of her jean shorts and checking the time. "What about you guys? When will you know?"

"Sometime tonight," Iggy says.

Maya plays with her bracelet. "I'm nervous."

"Don't be," Iggy says. "Lainey's right. You're really good."

"Good enough to beat you," Maya says, standing up and raising her eyebrows. She grabs a soccer ball off the deck.

"Is that a challenge?"

"I'm sure there wasn't a question mark at the end of my sentence."

Iggy grins. "Girls against boys."

"Let's do it." Maya turns to Lainey. "You've never played soccer until you've played alley soccer. It might even be better than the real thing. Come on!"

They head to the alley. "Where are the goals?" Lainey asks.

Malcolm drags two makeshift goals out of his garage. He and Iggy built them years ago. They're six feet across and four feet high. In the middle of each goal a pie tin dangles on a piece of twine. The only way to score is to make the pie tin ring. "In alley soccer there's no out of bounds," Malcolm explains to Lainey. "The ball is always in play."

Malcolm throws the ball in the air, and they're off. They chase after the ball as it bounces off garages, wooden fences, telephone poles, and garbage cans.

Iggy kicks the ball off his garage and straight into Mr. Johnson's wooden gate next door.

"You break that gate, you fix it!" Mr. Johnson hollers from his upstairs window.

"Sorry!" The boys are distracted long enough to let Maya slip past them to score the first goal. The pie tin rings, the sound echoing through the alley.

"What's the score?" Mr. Johnson yells.

"It's 1–0!" Maya shouts back.

They run up and down the alley, laughing and kicking the ball around. For a few minutes, they forget about tryouts and teams and just play soccer with no rules and a lot of fun.

THEY pause the game to move the nets out of the way as a car rolls down the alley.

Maya pulls her phone out again. " It's 5:45!" She looks at Lainey. "Almost time."

They end the game and head to the front of Malcolm's house to sit on the front steps. The girls look at their phones, waiting.

Refresh.

Refresh.

Refresh.

At 6:05 the Edison athletics web page freezes. Maya shakes her phone. "Come on! Come on!" Everyone is quiet for a moment, and then Maya screams. "The results are posted!"

Her face falls, but then she looks up as Lainey smiles. "We didn't make varsity, but at least we'll be together on JV."

"You should've made varsity, though," Lainey says.

"You should have too! But if we had, we'd just end up sitting on the bench as freshmen anyway. This is better. We'll get to play more." Maya and Lainey lean in together over their phones and talk about who made their team and who made varsity.

"Come on!" Malcolm checks his phone yet again. "Post the results already."

"No kidding."

As Iggy listens to Maya and Lainey talk, he feels increasingly nervous about how he did during tryouts and thinks about every mistake he made. His mind flashes back to Coach Yuro's face after he hit him with the soccer ball and then to Chad Swenson's face after Malcolm threw the slushy all over him. Iggy begins to wonder if either one of them has a chance to make varsity.

He looks down at his phone and presses Refresh again, but the screen turns black. His phone is dead.

"What time is it?" Iggy asks.

"It's 6:11," Malcolm says.

Maya looks up from her conversation with Lainey. "I should head home. I told my sister I'd help make dinner."

"Me too," Lainey says. "I need to tell my mom about tryouts!"

Iggy knows he'll be eating alone tonight. His mother picked up an extra shift at the hospital, and his father always works late on Friday nights. Iggy and Malcolm stand up and walk Maya and Lainey to the end of the yard.

"Text me when you guys know the results," Maya says.

"I have to plug in my phone first," Iggy says, showing her the blank screen.

"Wait!" Malcolm shouts, looking down at his phone. "Hold on! Hold on! The boys' rosters are up!" They crowd around him and look at his screen.

"Congratulations," Malcolm says, catching Iggy's eye. "You made varsity!"

"What?" Iggy is shocked. "No way."

Malcolm hands him the phone, and Iggy

sees his name on the varsity roster. Then he scans the rest of the list, but Malcolm's name isn't there.

"Click on the JV roster," Malcolm says nervously. "I can't look. What if Chad got me cut from the JV team too? The guy hates me."

"I doubt he has as much influence with the coaches as he thinks he does." Iggy clicks on the JV team, and his eyes scroll down the names.

"You're on JV," Iggy says. "But you should've made varsity. You're better than Smalley, and everyone knows it."

"I'm not bigger than him, though." Malcolm smiles, but it isn't his regular big grin. Iggy realizes that for the first time, they'll be on different teams.

"I'm good with JV," Malcolm says. "Really. I am. After today, I wasn't sure I'd make a team at all."

Iggy nods. "You and me both." They hang out on the steps awhile longer, dinner temporarily forgotten in the excitement.

"How did Chad make team captain anyway?" Malcolm asks, shaking his head.

"The guy is such a jerk." At that moment, a black convertible comes racing down the street.

Iggy looks at Malcolm and then at the black car. "You just said his name and conjured him. Spooky."

"If that's true, remind me to never say his name again."

The car screeches to a halt. "Watch out!" Iggy says, stepping in front of the girls. "They're armed with water balloons!"

The guys in the convertible laugh. Chad Swenson turns off the engine and slowly gets out.

"We come in peace," he says, walking toward them with his hands in the air. But when he draws near, he turns to Malcolm with an unpleasant gleam in his eye. "I guess you and I are even now. You dump on me, and I dump on you."

"He was the best goalie out there today," Iggy says.

Smalley gets out of the passenger seat of the convertible and stands there looming over everyone. "Coach Yuro didn't see it that way, freshman."

Chad takes a step closer to Malcolm and looks down at him. "I told Coach Yuro you reminded me of a leprechaun—small and green." He laughs, but Malcolm doesn't rise to the bait. He just looks down at his feet.

"You made a mistake if you want to win this year," Iggy says. "A big mistake."

"Come on, man, you scored on the kid." Chad tries to put his arm around Iggy's shoulders, but Iggy pulls away. "And no matter what I said, Coach Yuro wanted *you* on the team. I couldn't change his mind. So congrats to you. We came to welcome you to varsity. We're rounding up the new players and taking them out for a little fun."

Smalley gets back in the car and honks the horn. "Let's go!"

"Go where?" Iggy looks over at Malcolm, who won't meet his glance.

"Team bonding. But first, you need to put this on." Chad walks to the back of the convertible, grabs something wrapped in a plastic bag, and tosses it to Iggy.

Inside is a tiny, bright orange swimsuit.

"Nice!" Smalley calls. He and the other guys in the car roar with laughter.

"What are you going to make him do?" Maya asks.

"That's for us to know and Iggy to find out." Chad looks at Maya with interest. "Aren't you Lucy's sister?"

"Yeah," Maya replies, meeting his gaze and crossing her arms.

"You're almost as cute . . . almost." Chad grins, and the guys in the jeep all laugh again. Maya rolls her eyes.

Iggy steps between Maya and Chad. "What if I already have plans?"

"You don't have any plans," Malcolm says. "You should go." The words sound a bit flat.

"Hurry up!" Chad yells. "Get that thing on and get in this car. We've got places to go. Things to do!"

Iggy looks down at the orange suit. It's so small that he wonders if he'll be able to pull it on.

"You don't have to do this," Maya says.

"Yeah, I think I do," Iggy says. "If I don't go with them, I'll never be part of the team."

Smalley honks the horn again.

Iggy goes inside and puts on the suit. It's a struggle, but he managers to get it on. He wishes Malcolm had made the team more than ever. It would be nice to have his best friend along on this adventure.

He looks at himself in the mirror. *Yuck*, he thinks. Not only is it an ugly color, but it isn't even new. It's ratty and worn and very, very tight.

The car horn blares again from the street. Iggy sighs and pulls his soccer shorts on over the suit. He hopes all he'll have to do tonight is swim in a lake or maybe take a dip in a nasty swamp. But he has a feeling that's not the plan.

"Come on!" Chad yells as Iggy heads to the convertible.

Maya grabs his arm as he passes. "Be careful," she whispers. "I don't like that guy."

Malcolm pats him on the back. "Good luck!"

"Send us pictures," Lainey says with a laugh.

Iggy gets into the backseat, where he's crammed between two sophomores. As they drive away, Iggy looks over his shoulder and sees Malcolm, Lainey, and Maya watching him. For the first time, he wonders if he would be better off on the JV team.

CHAD drives downtown. Between the whipping wind and the music blasting from the sound system, Iggy can't hear a thing. But he can see Chad and Smalley talking and laughing up front.

The swimsuit cuts into Iggy's skin. He's never felt so uncomfortable in his life. Finally, Chad parks the car. They're in front of the art museum. Soon a couple more cars pull up, and more guys from the team get out.

"Welcome, newbies," Chad says. "Strip down to your suits and follow me."

Iggy takes off his sweatshirt and his shorts.

He looks at the other new members of the team—they're all wearing normal swim trunks, long and baggy and down to their knees. He's the only one in a tiny orange suit.

Chad takes out his phone. "Strike a pose," he says.

Iggy decides to go with it. He flexes his muscles like a bodybuilder and holds up his chin.

The new guys laugh, but Chad doesn't. He leads the group to a large water fountain in front of the museum. It's lit with bright lights, and Iggy can see coins littering the bottom—spare change that people have tossed in for wishes. If he had a coin to toss, he'd wish to be somewhere else right now.

Chad claps his hands to get their attention. "The object is to gather up enough loose change to buy each of the seniors a meal at Taco King."

"And I'm hungry!" Smalley says.

"You've got five minutes. Go!"

Iggy sits at the edge of the fountain, plugs his nose, and falls slowly backward like a scuba diver. The water is cold enough to make him gasp. But when he stands up, the new guys are laughing again.

Chad doesn't look amused. "Stop goofing around and find us some sunken treasure," he says.

Iggy starts splashing around. Goose bumps rise on his skin as his hands search the slimy, slippery fountain for coins. When he has a handful, he heads to the side and drops the change into a plastic bucket that Chad is holding.

"That should buy a taco or two," Chad says. "Keep going."

Iggy kicks his legs as fast as he can to stay warm. There are a lot of coins in the fountain, but most of them are pennies that he avoids. Finally, he gathers another handful of change and slogs toward the edge again.

Chad shakes the bucket. "Not enough," he says, but Iggy can see that the plastic bucket is more than half full and the other new guys are drying off. "Since you're the only freshman on the team, you need to prove that you belong." Chad stares at Iggy as he stands up in the fountain, daring him to protest.

"Fine." Iggy goes back in and splashes around. By now his skin is numb, and he doesn't feel the cold. He gathers another handful of change and resurfaces. But when he looks around, everyone is gone.

IGGY climbs out of the fountain and stands shivering in the night air. Someone has taken his clothes. They left his phone, but the battery is still dead.

He glances at the change in his hand and sees that he has just forty-five cents—not enough for bus fare. He considers heading back into the fountain and gathering more change, but then he remembers that all he's wearing is a tiny bathing suit. He's not going to ride the bus like that.

Iggy looks around the courtyard. He sees a man asleep on a bench and a couple who seem to be arguing about something. Then he spots a young family. The man is pushing a stroller, and the woman is holding a little boy's hand.

Advice from his mother pops into his head. "If you ever get lost or find yourself in trouble, look for someone with kids," she said. "People with children of their own will usually do all they can to help someone else's child."

Iggy calls out to the family. "Excuse me? Do you have a phone I could use? Someone took my clothes, and my phone is dead."

The man looks at him suspiciously, but the woman waves him over. She pulls a baby blanket from the bottom of the stroller and hands it to Iggy. He dries his hands and wraps the blanket around his shoulders. Then she hands him her phone.

"Are you OK?" she asks. He's shivering.

"I'll be fine. Thanks so much."

"What happened to your clothes?"

"It was just a prank." He tries to make it sound like no big deal, but the mother frowns.

"They just left you here?"

"I'm not sure. Maybe they'll be back?" Iggy looks around. "Maybe they left me a message, but my phone . . . the battery."

"Call your parents," the woman says. Iggy

nods, but he knows neither of his parents can just leave work. His father is the only person at the gas station, and his mother is in the middle of her shift.

He dials a number.

"Malcolm!" Iggy shouts when his friend picks up. He's never been so happy to hear Malcolm's voice in his entire life. "I need some help."

Fifteen minutes later, a small red car pulls up in front of the museum. Maya opens the front door, and Malcolm pulls himself out of the backseat and throws Iggy a warm sweatshirt and a pair of sweatpants.

"You're the best," Iggy says. He returns the wet baby blanket to the family and thanks them before hopping into the car.

Maya's sister Lucy is driving. "I owe you guys," Iggy says.

"No problem," Lucy says. "Nice suit."

"What happened?" Maya asks, and Iggy explains.

"Chad Swenson can be a complete jerk." Lucy shakes her head in the front seat. "He's the worst."

"Didn't he ask you out once?" Maya asks.

"I'd never go out with a guy like that. I've seen him bullying other kids since second grade."

Maya turns around and looks at Iggy. "I can't believe they just left you."

"When I get home, I'm going to give Chad a call," Lucy says. "You don't treat your teammates like that. That's not how you lead."

Iggy shakes his head. "Please, don't. I have to play with those guys, and I have a feeling Chad could make my life much worse."

"I agree." Malcolm looks at Iggy. "That guy has a vengeful streak."

"What goes around comes around," Maya says from the front seat. "You do bad things, and bad things happen to you. Just wait and see."

They arrive in their neighborhood and drop Iggy and Malcolm off.

"Do you want to come in?" Iggy asks. He wants to do something to thank them for saving him. "We have ice cream."

"I've got to go," Lucy says. "I'm heading to a party, but I'm sure Maya would love to hang out."

"Yeah, sure." Maya gives her sister a weird look.

"Ice cream!" Malcolm shouts, hurrying out of the car. "Do you still have that chocolate sauce your mom made the other day?"

"Yeah," Iggy says with a laugh.

Before they head to the kitchen, Iggy runs up to his room and changes into his own clothes.

"Better?" Malcolm asks when Iggy reappears.

"Yeah. Way better."

They head into the kitchen, and Iggy grabs the ice cream and three bowls. It occurs to him that he hasn't eaten dinner.

"Raspberry, chocolate chip, or vanilla?" he asks Maya.

"How about raspberry chocolate chip?"

"OK. That actually sounds really good." He plops a scoop of raspberry and then a scoop of chocolate chip into each of the bowls.

Malcolm's searching the fridge for toppings. He pours chocolate sauce and sprinkles into his bowl and adds whipped cream and strawberries. Then he digs in before even sitting down at the kitchen table.

"Slow down," Iggy laughs. Malcolm's cheeks are bulging like a chipmunk.

"So good," Malcolm mumbles.

"It is." Maya licks her spoon.

Iggy imagines the rest of the team at Taco King, enjoying their meal and laughing about how they left him behind with no clothes. "I wonder how many tacos they were able to buy with all the change I scooped up."

Maya squirts chocolate sauce into her bowl. "Did you feel bad about stealing all those wishes? A few of those pennies were probably mine. I always throw one in when we go to the museum."

"I guess I didn't even think about that," Iggy says, taking another bite. "I was focused on the fact that I was wading around a public fountain in a bright orange suit that barely covered my behind."

Maya and Malcolm laugh while Iggy, still hungry, gets up and turns on the oven. Then he grabs a pizza from the freezer.

The doorbell rings, and Iggy freezes.

"I texted Lainey while you were upstairs

changing," Maya says. "I hope you don't mind."

"No, not at all," Malcolm says in a rush before Iggy has a chance to reply. Iggy is just happy that it isn't Chad at the door with another "fun" activity planned.

They sit around the kitchen table and fill Lainey in on Iggy's night. They laugh and talk and eat slices of hot, gooey pizza. Iggy is happy and warm and glad he's at home instead of sitting around in a tight, wet bathing suit at Taco King.

SATURDAY is Iggy's first day of practice with the varsity team. He hasn't seen or spoken to any of his teammates since they left him looking for change in the water fountain. No one even texted to make sure he made it home.

He walks by himself to the field. It feels strange not to have Malcolm by his side. Being on different teams means they're on different schedules too.

Some guys are already on the field when Iggy gets there.

"Iggy the Piggy, you ditched us last night!" Chad shouts with that cocky half smile of his.

"*I* ditched *you?*" Iggy sits down on a bench and puts his cleats on. He's not thrilled with his new nickname.

"It was just a test," Chad says, putting his arm around Iggy's shoulders. "Did this little Iggy cry all the way home?"

"No." Iggy remembers what Maya said about Chad liking her sister. "Lucy Pham picked me up and gave me a ride home."

"Lucy?"

"Yeah," Iggy says, tying his shoe. "She's in your class. You don't know her?"

"I know her," Chad snaps. Then he moves closer and stands inches from Iggy. "Did you tell her it was my fault or your fault you got left behind?"

"What do you think?" Iggy asks. "How was it my fault?"

"You're a freshman. Everything is your fault. But seriously." Chad leans in toward Iggy. "I need you to tell Lucy I'm not a bad guy."

But you are a bad guy, Iggy thinks. He just looks at Chad.

"Here's what you're going to do," Chad says, still standing too close. "Next time you see her, put in a good word for me. Got it? Tell her what a great captain I am. Tell her she should go out with me."

She can't stand you, Iggy wants to say. Instead, he stands up. "Sure. Whatever."

"Good boy," Chad says, slapping him on the back as they head to the field.

Coach Yuro blows his whistle, and the team gathers around him. There aren't any introductions or words of welcome for the new players.

"You looked lazy during tryouts," Coach Yuro begins. "It's time to get into shape." His face is unmoving, and his eyes are like black pebbles as he paces back and forth in front of them. "I expect fierce players. I expect my team to win."

Coach Yuro has set up four sets of orange cones on the field. Iggy lines up with his team at one end of the field, and when Coach Yuro blows his whistle, they run to the first set of cones, touch the ground, and run back. They do this until they've hit them all. Then they do the whole thing again. Iggy feels as if he's going to puke, but he manages to keep his breakfast down. Two of the seniors aren't so lucky—they head to the side of the field and throw up.

Iggy's legs burn and his heart is pounding, but Coach Yuro doesn't give them much time to rest. For the next drill he lines up two dozen cones and has the players weave in and out between the cones while controlling a ball. If they lose control of the ball, they have to start again.

Finally, they pause for a water break. Iggy sits down on the bench and takes a huge swig from his bottle. Something solid hits his lips and falls into his mouth, and he leans forward and spits it out.

He takes the lid off the bottle and looks inside. He sees worms and dirt floating around.

A couple of seniors at the end of the bench look at each other and grin, and Chad laughs out loud.

Iggy raises his bottle and shouts, "Cheers!" He pretends to take a long drink. "Protein water! I heard worms are good for you."

He gets up and walks away from the field to a utility building with a water spigot on the side. Iggy dumps out the wormy water and rinses his bottle and adds fresh water. Then he takes a long, deep drink.

"What are you doing over there?" Coach Yuro yells.

"Just getting more water," Iggy shouts back. He knows Chad and the other guys are watching him. He doesn't say anything about the worms. He just takes another drink and heads back to the field, but the taste of worms and dirt lingers in his mouth.

AFTER practice, Iggy heads to Herbie's to work his shift. When he gets there, cars are lined up at the pumps, and someone is having problems with the car wash.

"Iggy!" His dad says. "Cover the register for me. I'll be right back."

Inside, Iggy grabs his work shirt, moves behind the counter, and begins ringing up customers.

Soon the bells on the door jingle, and Iggy sees Chad and a couple of other varsity players enter the store. They head straight to the slushy machine. Chad spills blue slushy on the floor and doesn't bother to wipe it up.

"What's up?" Chad says when he sees Iggy behind the counter. "You work here?"

"Yeah." Iggy rings up Chad's drink.

"Hold on." Chad grabs a bag of chips. "This too."

"$4.50," Iggy says.

"And this." He puts a pack of gum on the counter.

"$5.90." Iggy waits for Chad to pay, but he just stands there, sipping his drink. "Brutal practice, huh?"

"Yeah," Iggy says.

"I hope you know it wasn't me who put the worms in your water bottle. So don't go complaining to Coach Yuro or Lucy." Chad stares at Iggy and takes a long sip of his drink.

"I won't."

"I saw her after practice," Chad says. "She told me I needed to be nice to little Iggy Piggy. She seemed mad at me, and that's not good. I want to ask her to homecoming."

"That'll be $5.90," Iggy says again, but Chad still doesn't pay. He just stands there with a crooked smile on his face.

"Thanks for being such a good little freshman," Chad says finally. Instead of paying, he waves to the other guys, and they all walk out the door.

Iggy wants to run after them and make them pay. But he also wants to be accepted as a teammate. He's tired of being the odd man out.

"It's on me," Iggy says through his teeth as he takes cash out of his wallet for the four drinks, the bag of chips, and the gum.

Iggy's father comes back into the store a moment after Iggy puts the cash in the register. "Busy, busy," Mr. Baptiste says with a smile. "Business is good. So glad you're here to help."

"Yeah," Iggy says. "Business is great."

He slides his wallet into his back pocket. He can't tell his dad what just happened. These are his teammates—they're supposed to be on his side, and he's ashamed that they aren't.

"What's with the mess?" His father points to the spilled slushy on the floor.

"I'll get it." Iggy switches spots with his dad and cleans up.

The bell on the door rings again, and Iggy sees Malcolm, Lainey, and Maya enter the store.

"Hey!" Maya says. "Malcolm thought you might be working."

"Hello, Maya," Iggy's dad says.

"Hello, Mr. Baptiste." Maya introduces him to Lainey while Malcolm heads to the back of the store.

"We just stopped in to get a sports drink before practice," Malcolm explains.

"You practice together?" Iggy asks, looking at Maya and Lainey.

Maya nods. "Yeah. I guess the JV girls' and boys' teams practice together once a week. We're going to scrimmage today."

"And the girls are going to win," Lainey adds.

"Not with me in goal." Malcolm puts his money down on the counter.

"How was your first practice?" Maya asks Iggy as she pays for drinks for herself and Lainey.

"Brutal." Iggy feels the soreness in his thighs setting in. "We ran practically the whole time."

"Ouch," Malcolm says.

Iggy rubs his thighs. "Yeah, that sums it up."

"Well, we'd better get going," says Maya.

"Don't want to be late."

Iggy wants to tell his friends about what just happened with Chad, but he can't. Not with his dad standing right there. Instead, he just waves as they head out the door.

ON the first day of the new school year, Iggy is glad to see that he has the same lunch period as Malcolm, Maya, and Lainey. The four friends head to a table in the corner, but just as Iggy is about to sit down, Chad appears. He pokes Iggy in the shoulder. "You sit with the team." Chad points to a table on the other side of the cafeteria where the varsity soccer players are gathering.

Iggy looks at Malcolm.

"Go," Malcolm says.

"Yeah, I probably should."

Maya raises her right eyebrow. "So you only hang out with the varsity guys now?"

"No. But I should hang with them today. Maybe things will be better if they get to know me."

"Whatever," Maya says. "You don't have to do what that jerk tells you to do."

"He kind of does," Malcolm says, siding with Iggy. "Chad's the team captain."

Iggy nods. "Believe me, I'd rather eat with you, but if I don't go over there, it'll just make things worse for me at practice. The other day I drank worm water. I don't want to know what they'd do if I really made them angry."

"Gross," Lainey says.

Maya looks down at her food. "Well, then you'd better get going."

"By the way," Iggy says before leaving the table. "Warn your sister—Chad wants to ask her to homecoming."

"Yuck," Maya says. "That's grosser than drinking worm water."

"See you all later." Iggy walks over to sit with the team.

Chad pauses with a forkful of taco salad halfway to his mouth. "What took you so long?"

"I was talking to Lucy Pham's sister," Iggy says with a smile.

"Telling her what a great guy I am and how her sister should go out with me, I assume?"

"Yeah." Iggy takes a bite out of his sandwich. "Something like that."

When they're finished eating, the guys at the table get up and leave behind their garbage and trays.

"That's for you to clean up," Chad says before walking away. "Freshmen have to earn their keep."

Iggy looks at the table and considers just leaving the mess. Then he remembers the taste of the worm water and starts piling garbage on a tray. If he just plays along a little longer, maybe Chad and his friends will lay off.

Malcolm, Maya, and Lainey come over and help. "You don't have to," Iggy says. "This is my problem."

"The way they're treating you isn't right," Maya says.

"I know. But it's just temporary. I'm sure it'll get better soon."

"I hope so." Maya picks up a banana peel and tosses it onto a tray.

IGGY wakes up early on the morning of his first game. He's surprised to see his mother already up and making breakfast. She worked a double shift the day before and must be exhausted.

"You need a good breakfast," she says, cracking eggs into a pan. "It's a big day for you."

"You don't need to go," Iggy says. "I might end up riding the bench the whole game. You should stay home and sleep."

"No, no, no. I wouldn't miss your first varsity game for the world." She stirs the eggs and adds some cheese.

"Game day!" Iggy's father steps into the kitchen. "We've got something for you." From behind his back he produces a shoe box. Iggy opens it to reveal brand-new cleats.

"These are great!" Iggy sits down on a kitchen chair and slips the shoes on. They fit perfectly and are swimming-pool blue to match his uniform.

"Thank you," he says to his parents as he gives each of them a hug. "You didn't have to buy these. My old ones still work." He knows they've been saving money to buy Herbie's, and he feels guilty about the expensive shoes.

"You work hard for this sport," his mother says, fixing him a plate. "And we get to have some fun watching you play on the high school field with your new shoes. Now take them off before you scuff my kitchen floor."

"I've been told these shoes are guaranteed to score a goal!" His father laughs and messes up Iggy's hair.

"I'll try. These are definitely going to help." Iggy just hopes he gets into the game. He'd feel bad if he couldn't even step onto the field with his parents watching.

After breakfast, Iggy grabs his bag and his new shoes and heads out early so he can watch some of the JV soccer game. Malcolm makes a beautiful save early to rob the other team of a goal. He seems to know where the ball will go before it even leaves the player's foot.

All through the first half, Malcolm is a rock in the net. No one can score on him. He looks confident and focused. At halftime the Eagles have a commanding lead, 3–0. Iggy wishes he could stay until the end, but he has to head to the locker room to get ready for his game. Coach Yuro wants his players to be dressed and ready an hour before game time.

As Iggy heads toward the locker room, he notices Coach Yuro standing along the fence watching the JV game.

"They're looking good," Iggy says.

"We better look that good," Coach Yuro snaps. Then he turns and walks away.

IGGY sits on the bench at the beginning of
the varsity game, trying not to look up at his
parents—whenever he does, they wave to him.
The season gets off to an ugly start. The Eagles
make mistake after mistake, and they get scored
on just six minutes into the first half.

Smalley is tall and strong for a goalie, but
Iggy thinks he isn't half as good as Malcolm.
The guy doesn't know how to read the
field, and he didn't seem to notice the player
standing just to the left of the goal. Smalley
wasn't ready when the ball bounced in that
direction. The shot came in low and hard, and
he couldn't handle it.

After the Eagles are scored on a second
time, Iggy's teammates get frustrated and start

playing rough. Elbows and feet start flying. Chad nails an opposing player in the calf with his cleat. When the ref calls a penalty, Chad complains loudly enough that even the people in the bleachers can hear what he's saying. The ref gives him a yellow card.

As the game continues, Chad smashes into another player and holds up his hands as if it was an accident. It's obvious to Iggy that Chad was trying to knock the player down. Then two minutes before the end of the first half, Chad gets the ball and brings it down the field. He races past defenders trying to slow him down. The guy is fast. He's open in front of the net, but he overkicks the ball. It sails high above the top of the net.

At halftime, Coach Yuro makes them take a knee on the field. "Do you know what the greatest motivator in the world is?" the coach asks as he paces angrily in front of the team.

No one dares to say anything.

Coach Yuro pauses and looks at all of them, one by one. Then he resumes pacing. "Fear. Fear is the greatest motivator."

Iggy's eyes grow wide. *This guy is intense,* he thinks.

"So I am going to put some fear into you," the coach says. "If you don't perform well out there—starting now—I move you down to the JV team and move some of the JV players up. Got it?"

"Yes, sir," they all say.

For a second, Iggy thinks maybe this is what he's been waiting for—maybe he'd be better off on the JV team. But then he looks over and sees his parents in the stands and remembers how proud of him they were that morning, and he knows that he can't just give up. He won't let them down.

"You." Coach Yuro points to Iggy. "Get out there. Take Swenson's place. He needs to cool down."

Chad scowls when he hears this. He throws his towel to the ground and shoves another player out of the way as he takes a seat on the bench.

The second half begins much like the first ended, with the Eagles playing defensively.

Then Iggy steps in front of a pass, traps the ball, turns quickly, and makes his way down the sideline. He spots one of his teammates wide open near the goal and hits him with a pass. The teammate puts his shot past the goalie for the Eagles' first goal of the season. The hometown crowd goes wild, and when Iggy looks in that direction, he sees Malcolm, Maya, and Lainey cheering near the fence.

Coach Yuro keeps Iggy out there for the rest of the game, and he plays hard. The Eagles score again to tie it, and with twenty seconds left in regulation time, Iggy takes a pass in front of the goal. With defenders closing in fast, he doesn't have time to aim his shot, but the ball rockets into the top right corner of the net, just past the goalie's fingertips. The Eagles hold on to win the game.

"That's how you play soccer!" Back in the locker room, Coach Yuro still seems angry, despite the win. "Maybe this team needs a few more freshmen like Iggy? What do you think?"

The team is silent. Coach Yuro's plan to motivate them with fear worked, but no one seems happy about it. Instead of the usual buzz of excitement after winning a game, instead of heading out together to get pizza to celebrate, the players quietly go their separate ways. Iggy ends up walking home by himself.

AFTER practice the next day, Iggy notices some of the guys snickering in the locker room. He tries to ignore it, but when he opens his locker door, he finds out quickly what they're laughing about.

The smell hits him first. Someone put roadkill in his locker—something furry and flat that has been baking on a hot asphalt road. Iggy's face flushes. He's had enough of the jokes and the pranks. He grabs the thing by its tail and flings it at the group of guys standing a few feet away.

It hits Chad in the face. He screams and spits and runs to the showers. The other guys laugh, this time at Chad.

Iggy grabs a towel and picks the roadkill off

the floor. Before he throws it away, he turns to his teammates. "Maybe I should save this for Chad? Do you think he wants to take it home?"

Most of the guys laugh again, but Smalley looks serious. He catches Iggy's eye. "You better get out of here. I'd be gone before Chad gets out of the shower."

Iggy takes his advice. He gathers his things and heads for home, cutting through alleys and avoiding sidewalks. He keeps looking over his shoulder for Chad's black convertible.

THAT night Malcolm and Maya hang out at Iggy's house, talking and doing their homework around the kitchen table. "A dead squirrel?" Maya asks. "Really?"

"Maybe a possum," Iggy says. "Or a rabbit? I don't know. I didn't look too closely, and it was flattened. Shoveled straight off the road. Totally disgusting."

"What did you do?" Malcolm asks.

Iggy tells them about throwing the dead animal at Chad, and they laugh when he imitates Chad's scream.

"I don't think this is the end of it, though" Iggy says. "I'm sure he's not going to let this go."

"Maybe it's time to say something to your coach," Maya says, twisting her hair into a bun and stabbing a pencil through it to keep it on top of her head.

"I don't know," Iggy says. "Coach Yuro isn't the type of guy you talk to. About anything."

"Maybe talk to Coach Julio, then," Malcolm says. "He listens to us. He told us his door is always open."

Iggy decides to change the subject. "So how was your practice?"

They tell him about their day. It sounds like a fun practice, much more laid back than what Iggy's used to with the varsity team. Hearing about it doesn't make him feel any better.

They're quietly working on their homework when Malcolm's phone buzzes.

"Iggy," Malcolm says, holding up his phone. "You won't believe who just texted me!"

Iggy squints and tries to read the text from across the table.

"Coach Yuro!" Malcolm shouts excitedly. "He wants me to practice with you guys tomorrow! What does that mean? Do you think he wants me to move up?"

Iggy's face falls, and Maya nudges him under the table.

"That's great," Iggy says, forcing his face into a grin. "Yeah. Great. Coach Yuro said something about moving players up."

He doesn't explain the threat Coach Yuro made about moving varsity players down. He doesn't explain how this could get really ugly really fast with the upperclassmen. Iggy knows there are guys on his team who will turn on anyone who moves up—and Chad will be leading them.

"What?" Malcolm says, looking at Iggy. "You don't seem that excited for me."

"I am!" Iggy forces another smile. "No, really, I am. We'll be on the same team. Just like old times."

AFTER school, Iggy and Malcolm walk to
practice together. It's nice to be on a team
with his friend again, but as soon they get to
the locker room, Iggy knows things aren't
going to be good.

"What's *he* doing here?" Chad scowls. "The
little boys don't practice until later."

"I'm practicing with varsity today,"
Malcolm says. He sounds nervous. "Coach
Yuro texted me last night."

Chad is silent for a moment. Then he looks
at two seniors leaning against their lockers.

"Who played a joke on this kid?"

One of the guys laughs.

"Come on. Who sent this kid a text making
him think he can play with us?"

The seniors shrug. "Not us," one of them says.

"He's good," Iggy says, loud enough for everyone in the locker room to hear. "He's fast. The first two games he's played for JV have both been shutouts."

Quiet falls over the locker room. Someone coughs.

Chad moves closer to Malcolm. "Go home," Chad says.

Smalley gets up and stands next to Chad. The big goalie towers over Malcolm. "Yeah, Coach Yuro never said anything to me about moving down."

Malcolm looks at Iggy.

"Show them the message," Iggy says.

Malcolm takes out his phone, and Chad whacks it out of his hand. It hits the bench, and the screen cracks. Malcolm picks it up.

"Look what you did," he says.

"Not my fault," Chad says. "It's your fault for showing up here today. What are you doing here? No one wants you on this team."

"I do," Iggy says.

"That's because no one here likes you either."

Suddenly Coach Yuro pounds on the locker room door. "Hurry it up! I want you on the field in three minutes. Move it! You're all wasting my time."

Everyone hurries to get dressed.

"What if it is just a joke?" Malcolm whispers to Iggy as he ties his cleats. "What if someone is just messing with me."

"It's not a joke," Iggy says in a hushed voice. "You're better than Smalley. I know it. Coach Yuro knows it. Even Chad and Smalley know it. Don't listen to them."

They get up to leave, but Chad and two other seniors are blocking the door.

"Where are you going?" he says to Malcolm.

"To the field," Malcolm says.

"No." Chad grins. "You're going to go home, or you're going to go for a little swim. Headfirst. Your choice." He nods to the toilet stall.

Iggy's temper rises, and he shoves Chad in the chest. Chad stumbles backward, but he recovers quickly and is ready to fight. One of the seniors grabs Iggy and puts him in a headlock. Malcolm is about to jump on the senior's back when Coach Yuro sticks his head back into the locker room.

"What's going on in here?" He shouts. "I thought I told you to get to the field."

Chad glares at Malcolm. The guy holding Iggy lets go, and Malcolm backs off.

"I said, what's going on?" Coach Yuro says. "Now answer me."

Chad points at Malcolm. "We're just worried this little freshman is too tiny to practice with us. We wouldn't want to hurt him."

"Enough of this fooling around," Coach Yuro snarls. "Get out there."

Chad and the other guys head down the hall toward the field.

Malcolm lingers. Iggy can tell he's nervous.

"Do you want me out there too?" Malcolm asks Coach Yuro.

"Do you want to be out there?"

"Well, yeah," Malcolm says.

"Then go show me you can handle those guys!"

After running sprints, Coach Yuro calls the team together on the field. "We're going to have a little shootout. The goalie who makes the most saves starts the game on Saturday."

As they take their places on the field, Iggy hears Chad talking to Smalley. "We've got your back, man. No way this little freshman is going to take your place."

Everyone lines up. Malcolm is first in the net.

Chad moves to the front of the line. "You're going down," he says. Chad takes three steps and gives the ball a powerful kick. It curves to the right, but Malcolm is ready. He pounces and punches the ball into the air, deflecting it over the net. No goal.

Iggy is up next. Part of him wants Malcolm to stay on JV. He doesn't want his best friend to have to deal with Chad and the other varsity players. Iggy gives a slight nod to the right. He sees Malcolm shift in that direction, but at the last second Iggy pivots and shoots left. Malcolm is quick as lightning and almost gets to the ball anyway, but he misses it by a few inches. Goal.

Iggy goes to the back of the line without looking at Malcolm. He doesn't want to see the look on his friend's face.

Iggy soon realizes that if he wanted to keep Malcolm off varsity, tricking him like that was probably a bad idea. Iggy's goal just made Malcolm angry and more determined than ever—and he needs that determination, because every player takes his best shot at him. Malcolm stops a dozen shots and only lets in a few.

Smalley doesn't do as well even though his friends take it easy on him. He covers a lot of the goal, but he's lumbering and not quick on his feet. He lets five shots get past him, including a couple of easy ones that he should have stopped. He looks mad when it's over. Really mad. Iggy watches Chad talking to Smalley on the sideline. The huge goalie looks over at Malcolm and laughs as Chad flashes his crooked grin. Iggy feels a chill run down his spine.

Iggy finds Malcolm after practice. "What was that about?" Malcolm asks. He looks really mad.

"They're out to get you," Iggy says. "You need to be careful."

"No," Malcolm shouts. "You're the one out to get me!" Iggy is shocked at how upset his friend is. "I thought you were on my side, and you intentionally faked me out. What's your problem? You think you're the only freshman good enough for the varsity team? You think I don't belong?"

"No, that's not it." Iggy tries to explain, but Malcolm cuts him off.

"Friends don't do what you just did to me. You know how much I want to make this team, and you tried to sabotage me in front of everyone. I could tell you didn't want me here when I got the text from Coach Yuro last night. I don't need your help, so just stay away from me!" Malcolm turns and walks away.

Iggy starts to go after him, but Coach Yuro calls him over.

"You're going to start the game tomorrow," Coach Yuro says. Then he starts talking about strategy, but Iggy only half listens to him. He notices Maya and Lainey make their way down to the field. They stop and talk to Malcolm.

Iggy realizes Malcolm is smart enough not

to go back into the locker room until the rest of the guys have cleared out. He lingers outside with Maya and Lainey.

Coach Yuro snaps his fingers in Iggy's face. "Repeat back to me what I just told you." He knows Iggy wasn't paying attention.

"I . . ." Iggy mumbles.

Yuro cuts him off. "Never mind. I'm benching you until you can show me some respect."

Iggy starts to explain that he's worried about Malcolm, but Coach Yuro yells for Chad, who has just emerged from the locker room. "What's up, Coach?"

"You're back in the starting lineup for tomorrow's game."

Chad brushes past Iggy and grins. "See? There's no way you and your little friend are going to take any starting spots on this team. Remember that."

Iggy glares at Chad before turning to his friends. "Hey!" He waves to Malcolm, Maya, and Lainey.

Maya waves back. "We're late for practice!

We'll talk to you later." Then they disappear into the school.

Malcolm doesn't wait for him. He heads into the locker room, and just as Iggy is heading through the door, Malcolm is heading out. He didn't bother to change. He just grabbed his stuff and left.

"Hey," Iggy says. "Wait up. I'll be right back out. I want to talk to you."

Iggy knows not to linger in the locker room either. He grabs his stuff and hurries out before Chad comes back. But when he gets outside, Malcolm is gone.

MALCOLM won't answer Iggy's texts. When Iggy gets home, he goes next door and knocks on the door, but no one answers. He decides to give Malcolm some space. Iggy is scrolling through his phone a few hours later when he sees a photo Lainey posted of herself, Malcolm, and Maya eating ice cream.

No one invited him. Then he notices a photo of most of his teammates gathered at Chad's house, swimming in his pool.

Iggy's never felt so alone. He walks down to Herbie's and sits with his dad for a while.

"You look tired," his dad says.

"I am." He's tired of having to battle his own teammates. He's tired of being a bad best friend.

"You need to get some rest," his father says. "Big game tomorrow."

Iggy is considering telling his dad about what's been going on with his teammates and with Malcolm when a group of customers walks in. The store suddenly becomes busy. Iggy pitches in, and when the customers leave, he helps his dad stock the shelves. He feels a bit better after working for an hour.

"Now head home and get some rest," his father says. "Your mother and I will be there to cheer for you tomorrow."

"I thought you worked on Saturdays," Iggy says.

"I got someone to cover for me. There's no way I'm going to miss your games if I can help it."

When Iggy heads home, he grabs his soccer ball and goes out to the alley. He drags one of the goals out and shoots over and over again. The pie tin rings, but the sound seems empty out there by himself.

"You're keeping me up!" Mr. Johnson yells out his window. "Knock it off."

"Sorry!" Iggy saw the light go on in Malcolm's room a few minutes ago. He was hoping the sound of the pie tin would draw him out, but it didn't.

Iggy heads inside and goes to bed, but he just lays there staring at the ceiling. He gives up on sleep and tries to text Malcolm again.

I'm sorry, he writes. *I know you'll do great tomorrow.*

A few minutes later, his phone buzzes and Iggy grabs it from his nightstand.

"Are you up?" The text isn't from Malcolm. It's from Maya. Instead of responding, he turns his phone off and rolls onto his side.

IGGY walks to the soccer field alone. He knocked on Malcolm's door before he left, but no one answered. Iggy looks for him in the locker room, but he's not there yet.

He gets dressed and sends Malcolm another message. *Where are you?* The rest of the team is already there. Soon Coach Yuro will walk through the door, and anyone who isn't there yet won't get to play.

"Anyone see Malcolm?" Iggy asks. He looks around the room, but no one says anything.

Chad slams his locker closed. "If he doesn't show, Coach Yuro will make him pay for it." He smiles with his usual uneven grin, and Iggy sees him catch Smalley's eye. Iggy realizes they must have done something to make Malcolm late.

Iggy calls Malcolm, but the call goes right to voice mail.

He tries another text. *Where are you??????*

Iggy paces around the locker room. He hears Coach Yuro in the hallway and notices Chad checking his watch.

Just then, Malcolm stumbles through the door. He looks unsteady on his feet, and his face is pasty white.

"What did you do to him?" Iggy says, looking at Chad.

Chad shrugs. "We took him out for breakfast. Welcomed him to the team. We treated him right." He laughs. "We dropped him off at home to get his stuff, and he said he was feeling a little tired, that he wanted to walk to the game to wake up. Isn't that right, little buddy?" Chad puts his arm around Malcolm.

"What?" Malcolm asks. He looks confused. He doesn't look like himself, not at all. "I don't feel right."

"You must have eaten something rotten," Chad says in his best concerned voice. "Or maybe you're just nervous about playing with the big guys. Nerves will get you every time."

Malcolm sits down on a bench, and Iggy gets him a cup of water.

Just as Coach Yuro barrels into the room, Malcolm throws up. Then he slumps over and falls to the floor, unconscious.

"Someone call an ambulance!" Iggy shouts. "Call 911!"

THE paramedics arrive quickly, but
Malcolm is unresponsive.

"He's having trouble breathing!" One of
the paramedics puts a mask over Malcolm's
mouth and begins pushing oxygen into his
lungs. They load him onto a stretcher and
rush him out of the room to the ambulance
parked outside.

Iggy follows and sees the red and blue
lights on the ambulance come to life. Then
he watches as the ambulance pulls away, its
siren screaming.

Iggy runs to the stands. He finds his
parents sitting next to Malcolm's mother, and
he tells them what just happened. They rush to
the parking lot and jump into his father's car.

They arrive at the hospital just minutes after the ambulance delivered Malcolm to the ER.

After a nurse leads Malcolm's mother through two gray doors, Iggy looks around in anguish. "What do we do?" He feels desperate to take action.

"We wait," Iggy's mother says. "We just have to wait and stay calm." They head to a pale-green room with a fish tank in one corner. Iggy stares at the fish as they make their circuit around the tank, but he doesn't really see them.

Maya and Lainey arrive a few minutes later. The news that Malcolm collapsed is spreading fast.

"When they called off the game, I knew something was really wrong," Maya says. "I heard the ambulance, but I had no idea who was in it at first. What happened?"

"I don't know for sure," Iggy says. "But he was with Chad and some of the other guys this morning. I know they did something to him." In his mind he sees Malcolm slumping over and sliding to the floor. He can't stop replaying the scene over and over.

Just then, Coach Yuro appears in the waiting room. Chad and Smalley and some of the other players are with him.

"What did you do to him?" Iggy springs across the room, but Coach Yuro cuts him off. All the fear and anger he's been holding in erupts. He knows this is Chad's fault. He can see it in his face. "What did you do?" he yells again.

"Hold on," Coach Yuro says. "What makes you think Chad had something to do with this?"

Iggy turns to the coach with tears in his eyes. "Chad and his friends have been terrorizing me for weeks. Now they've started in on Malcolm, and I know they caused this somehow."

Iggy turns to Chad, who slumps into a chair next to the fish tank.

"What did you do?" Iggy says slowly and steadily. "Tell me right now." He's clenching his jaw and his fists.

Chad just shakes his head. But then Smalley speaks up. "Chad gave him . . . an energy drink, he called it," Smalley says quietly. Chad glares at him, but Smalley keeps going. "He told Malcolm it would help him focus and get rid of his nerves. Chad told him it was just cherry juice and honey and all natural stuff, but he spiked it with cough medicine. The nighttime stuff. I told him not to do it, but Chad said it would make him sleepy. That's all. He wanted him to make enough mistakes so that Coach Yuro would pull him. He was trying to get me back in the net."

Coach Yuro's face is more animated than Iggy has ever seen it. He looks scared. "Where's the doctor?" he shouts.

"Malcolm and his mom went through the doors at the end of the hall," Iggy's father says.

Iggy follows Coach Yuro and his father into the hallway. The coach heads for the doors. A nurse tries to stop him, but the coach ignores him and bursts through.

Iggy and his father are left alone in the hallway. Iggy wants to rush in there too. He wants to be with his friend. "Hang in there, buddy," his father says. He puts his arm around Iggy's shoulders. "Malcolm's going to be OK."

A nurse escorts Coach Yuro back to the waiting room. He looks at Chad, who stands up quickly.

"The kid is allergic to codeine," Coach Yuro says. "There was codeine in that cough syrup. What you gave him, his body couldn't handle."

"What?" Chad says. He's shaking. His face is white. He sits back down.

"I told the doctor what you gave him, but Malcolm's in bad shape right now."

"It was just cold medicine. I didn't think it would hurt him."

"But it did," Iggy says quietly. "It did."

EVERYONE in the waiting room is quiet and still, except for Iggy. He paces, and when he feels as if he can't take it anymore, he walks over to Chad and stands over him.

"If Malcolm doesn't recover . . ." Iggy says.

Maya moves next to Iggy and touches his arm. "Chad," she says. "I think you should go home."

Chad's eyes are red, and he's still trembling. "I need to stay. I can't leave." He puts his head in his hands and sobs.

Iggy goes into the hallway. He paces and stares at the doors where they took Malcolm. Ten minutes pass. Twenty.

Maya and his mother take turns trying to comfort him. They ask him to come back into the waiting room, but he can't be in the same place with Chad. He can't sit still.

Then Coach Yuro approaches Iggy. "I'm sorry," the coach says. "This is partly my fault. I pitted teammates against teammates. I should have been promoting teamwork, but instead, I had you at one another's throats."

"Malcolm just wanted to play with the varsity team," Iggy says. "That's all. He just wanted to play."

Iggy sees Coach Yuro's face crack. His usual hard expression is gone. He sees sadness and regret in the coach's eyes. Coach Yuro shakes his head. "I'm so sorry this happened, but Malcolm is going to pull through. He's a tough kid."

"He's not just going to pull through, he's going to play again," Iggy says. "He has to."

A wave of exhaustion overcomes Iggy. He leans into Maya, who is suddenly at his side again. She takes his hand and leads him back into the waiting room, far away from Chad.

"Sit," Maya says, and Iggy falls into a chair.

Twenty more minutes pass that feel like twenty hours. Finally, a nurse leads Malcolm's mother into the waiting room. She's crying, and Iggy's heart flops in his chest.

"He's going to be OK," she says, laughing and crying at the same time. "They got him here in time." She looks at Iggy and smiles through her tears. "He's going to be OK. He just needs to rest."

Iggy feels tears running down his face, but he doesn't bother to wipe them away. When he finally lifts his head and looks around the room, he sees that both Chad and Coach Yuro are gone.

TWO weeks later, Iggy and Malcolm walk to the soccer field together. The weather has cooled, and the smell of fallen leaves is in the air.

"I'm glad you're finally back in action," Iggy says.

"Me too." Malcolm seems as healthy as ever. "I can't wait to get back out there."

They walk in silence for a few minutes until Iggy stops and looks at Malcolm. "I want you to know, when I nodded right but kicked that ball to the left, it wasn't because I didn't want you on the team. I love playing with you. I did it because being on that team wasn't fun. It was ugly. Every day in the locker room, on the field, everywhere, it was never fun."

Malcolm nods. "I know. I knew soccer could be rough on the field sometimes, but I never thought it could be so rough off the field too."

"It's going to be better now that Chad is off the team," Iggy says. "And Coach Yuro has changed too. Practices are more fun. He's actually encouraging us out there."

"Good." Malcolm kicks a small stone on the sidewalk. It skitters across the white concrete. "I guess everything turned out OK." They catch up to the stone, and Malcolm kicks it again. "I feel bad for the guy, though," he says.

"Chad? Why? He almost killed you."

"Because I'm here," Malcolm says. "Heading to the soccer field with my best friend. We're freshmen with the whole season ahead of us and more seasons after that, and Chad is a senior who just threw away his last chance to play."

"Do you think guys like that change?" Iggy asks as they reach the field.

"Look at Coach Yuro," Malcolm says, and Iggy nods. "If someone like him can change, there's hope for anyone."

When they get to the locker room, the other guys welcome Malcolm and tell him they're glad he's OK. They're glad he's on the team. Iggy sits down next to his friend as they put on their cleats. Iggy smiles when he sees Malcolm's shoes. They're cleaned and polished and once again a bright, bold red.

GRIDIRON

THE CLUTCH

PAUL HOBLIN

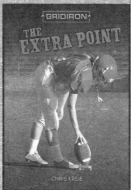

THE EXTRA POINT

CHRIS KREIE

FALSE START

PAUL HOBLIN

THE LATE HIT

K. R. COLEMAN

SHOWDOWN

K. R. COLEMAN

SIGNING DAY

K. R. COLEMAN

Leave it all on the field!

ABOUT THE AUTHOR

K. R. Coleman is a teacher at the Loft Literary Center in Minneapolis, Minnesota. Recently, she was awarded a Minnesota State Arts Board Grant and Sustainable Artist Grant. She lives in Minneapolis with her husband, two boys, and two dogs named Happy and Gilmore.